LOVE, DELIVERED

LOVE ON SUNDOWN
BOOK ONE

NORA LANE

First edition. February 2026

Cover Design by Leigh Jones of @storiesbyleigh

Character Art by Gabriela Rey (@madameardent)

Editing by Elena with Page and Polished

Interior Formatting by Nora Lane of @noralanewrites

ISBN (paperback): 979-8-9932867-3-0

ISBN (ebook): 979-8-9932867-2-3

 Formatted with Vellum

BLURB

Sara Mei Lin is perfectly content living life indoors—streaming League of Legends to thousands of viewers, surviving on late-night deliveries, and keeping her heart safely guarded after a devastating betrayal.

The outside world is optional. DoorDash is not.

What Sara doesn't know is that her preferred Dasher, Dave, is the neighbor she's been crushing on.

Dave Francis Rosenberg signs up to be a Dasher as a distraction from the pressure of respiratory therapy school—not to catch feelings. But when one customer's orders come with witty banter and an unexpected spark, Dave finds himself looking forward to every notification.

As messages turn flirtatious and boundaries blur, Dave must decide if he's brave enough to step out from behind the screen and confess the secret he's been hiding—or if his self-doubt will cause him to lose the girl he's been yearning for.

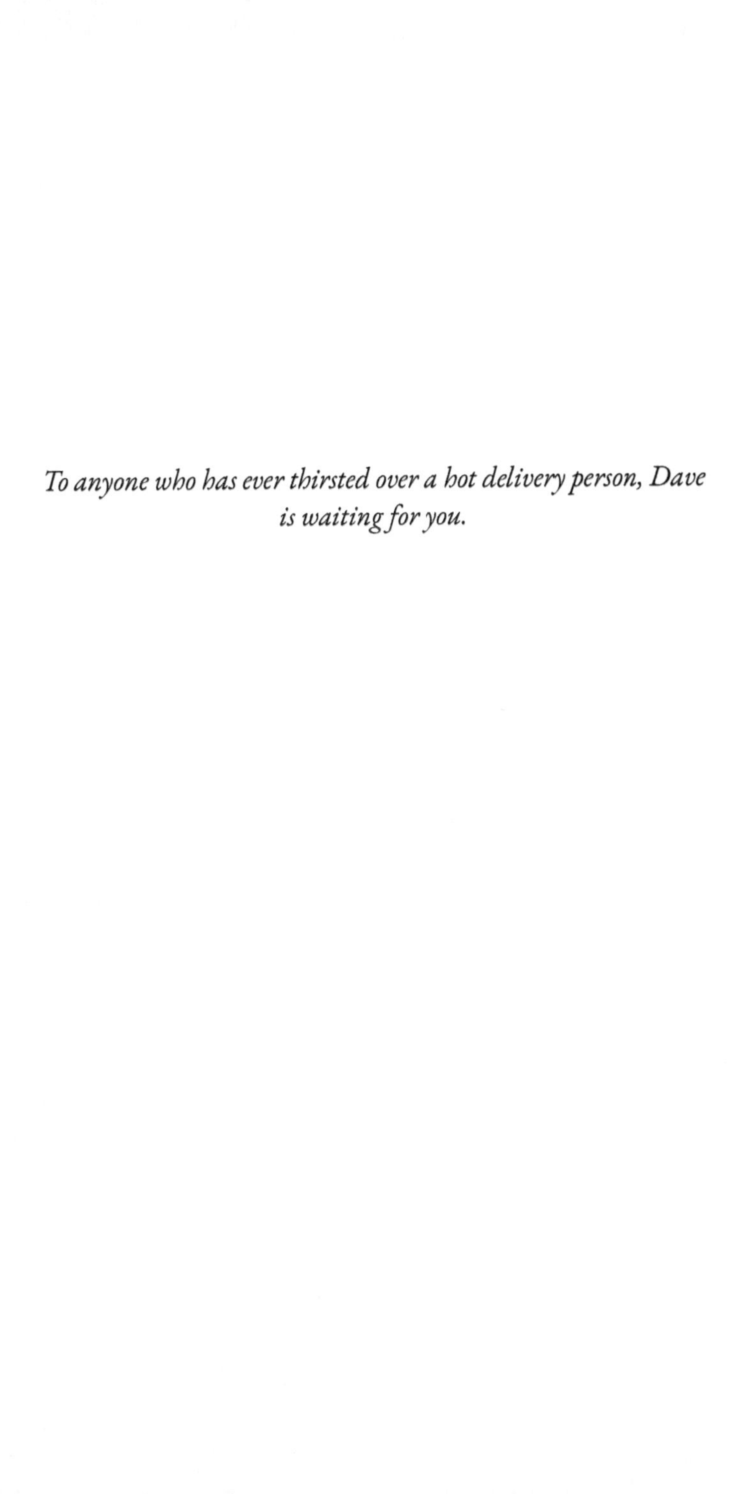

To anyone who has ever thirsted over a hot delivery person, Dave is waiting for you.

AUTHOR'S NOTE

Dear, Reader!

Thank you for taking a chance on Love, Delivered!

If this is your first book by me, welcome to my little corner of books. I like to write bite size love stories that gives you all the giggles and swoon.

Love, Delivered is a heartwarming holiday romance about a cinnamon roll DoorDash driver who finally gets a chance with the reclusive girl next door, who he has been yearning for since their first meeting. This fast-paced, low-drama, and light-hearted story will end in a guarantee HEA.

Love, Delivered is my first sweet and spicy novella. It contains explicit sexual content, profanity, mention of lung cancer and the death of grandparents.

If all the above aligns with you, then buckle up and be prepare to fall for the hot delivery guy.

With love,
Nora

PLAYLIST

Nothin' Like You - **Dan + Shay**
I'm Sprung - **T-Pain**
Always On Time - **Ja Rule ft Ashanti**
Best Friend - **Saweetie ft Doja Cat**
Body Language - **Jesse McCartney**
When Did You Get So Hot? - **Sabrina Carpenter**
With You - **Chris Brown**
Wi$h Li$t - **Taylor Swift**

CONTENTS

1

DAVE

"Pocketful of Sunshine" has got to be the catchiest song of the early two-thousands. I hum to myself as I cruise the aisles of Target between study sessions. It's eleven at night on a Friday, and while some people unwind with a drink, I find comfort in leisurely browsing the aisles, letting my mind wander aimlessly. Last semester, I decided to put my mindless strolling to good use and became a Dasher. It was the best decision, I got to destress and make some extra cash. Financial Independence, Retire Early life here I come.

I head to the refrigerated section, checking my phone for confirmation. I scan the milk selection a few times before messaging my customer.

DAVE

Hi, this is Dave, your DoorDash shopper. Your oat milk is out of stock, but this brand has better ratings.

sends picture of oat milk carton

If you want, I can grab this one instead.

I pocket my phone and head toward the cereal aisle, contemplating if I overstepped. I mean, I sent two messages about oat milk. Usually, when an item is out of stock and the customer hasn't provided a substitution, I'm supposed to mark it as unavailable and move on, but I can't help it—it's the people-pleaser in me. I want to make sure the person on the receiving end is happy, even if it's just a simple grocery delivery.

I'm browsing the cereal selection, double-checking my app to verify the right size, when I feel a tug on my jacket. I glance down to see chubby fingers tugging at a sticker stuck to the elbow of my jacket. I smile at the gesture and find innocent hazel eyes staring back at me.

His mom hasn't noticed our interaction yet; she's focused on deciding between Apple Jacks or Froot Loops, and I don't blame her, it's the *Sophie's Choice* of cereal options. Her blonde hair is pulled up into a high ponytail, and she's wearing workout clothes paired with tennis shoes, which is practical for having a toddler. You need to be quick and adaptable to catch them because they're wildly unpredictable. She reminds me of my sister, Eliana, who's always multitasking. I'd bet she's the eldest daughter type—the one who wants to take care of everyone. Eliana's only six years older than me, but at thirty-three sometimes she feels more like a second mom than a sister. She's always calling to check in and make sure that I eat, or asking if I'm seeing anyone.

The toddler—maybe two—sitting in the cart's baby seat, with an open box of animal crackers. Ten bucks says he threw a tantrum and she caved. Honestly, no judgment from me— I've opened a bag of chips while shopping more times than I can count. If adults with twenty-plus years of life experience can snack mid-store, then toddlers who can't even wipe their own asses definitely get a pass.

He reaches out trying to grab the sticker on my elbow

again. I take pity on him and pull it off, handing it over. I'm rewarded with a wide grin. He reminds me of my nephew: same mischievous little smile, hazel eyes, blonde curls flopping over his forehead. No doubt this sticker is from the last time I saw him. I return the toddler's smile, focusing back on my cereal selection, making a mental note to call my sister and offer to babysit my nephew one of these days. I'm sure she and her husband, Josh, could use some time off from the little gremlin.

I'm rearranging the handheld basket to fit all four boxes of cereal when a message buzzes through.

SARA

Yes, that would work. Milk and cereal are a necessity—please substitute with whatever is available.

I glance down at the four boxes of cereal she has on her list: Corn Pops, Cap'n Crunch, Frosted Flakes, and Honey Bunches of Oats. A very solid—and very chaotic—variety.

DAVE

I'm on it for the milk. As for the cereal, everything was in stock. Very wide range of options.

SARA

Perfect!! I need different ones for every mood. You never know what the night has in store.

The night? I pause, curious what she means, but I don't want to come off weird. I'm here to do a job, not treat this like a dating app. Still... curiosity wins. Before I can lose my nerve, I fire off a quick message.

DAVE

The night? What are you—some kind of astrology-coded moon gremlin powered by the tides?

SARA

Hahaha, 'moon gremlin,' I guess yes and no. I do believe when Mercury is in retrograde, I am at my worst, but the cereal consumption is not impacted by the moon. It's more like…

I need different types of sugar and crunch to keep my edge.

Her response raises at least a dozen questions, but I try not to be creepy, so I let the conversation die and move on to finding the rest of her order.

Twenty minutes later, I drive down a familiar street and pull up to the cute little cottage-style house catty-corner from mine. As I sit in front of the house, staring blankly, I start to wonder if *fate* is real.

If you'd told me when I became a Dasher that I'd be delivering groceries to the neighbor I've been crushing on for the last five years, I would've said you were lying. But in a weird twist of fate, here I am hovering outside her door with her groceries.

I grab my phone and step out of the car, her groceries balanced in my arms, and pause to take it all in. Her cottage radiates warmth before I even reach the porch—soft lights illuminating the pathway and a seasonal wreath on the door.

When I saw her name and address appear on the delivery app, it felt like kismet. I know it might sound strange, but having the safeguard of the delivery app made it easier to start anew and forget about the mistakes of the past.

It's been five years since I first laid eyes on Sara, yet the memory is still fresh, as if it never left. That summer had been hotter than the Devil's balls. I've lived in Eagleton, Oklahoma, my whole life, and when you've been here long enough, you learn to endure the heat and humidity—but she made it harder to ignore.

She wore jean shorts and a white tank top that showed off her dainty frame, wrought with curves in all the right places—places I wanted to sink my teeth into. Literally. The kind of woman wet dreams are made of. I spotted her beside the open moving truck, wrestling boxes into her arms with more determination than skill.

Her short black hair skimmed her shoulders, half pulled back into a loose, careless bun. A few strands escaped, catching the light as she moved. When her deep brown eyes lifted and met mine, it was like gravity locked me in place and I found myself transfixed by her beauty. And then she rewarded me with the most beautiful smile I've ever seen. One that seemed to radiate from the inside out. I swear my heart skipped a beat. I should've gone over and introduced myself, or offered to help with her boxes. Instead, I stood there like an idiot, staring at a woman so far out of my league we weren't even in the same galaxy.

A few weeks later, our neighborhood busybody, Sue, decided to host *Sunrise on Sundown*, a breakfast block party. There was coffee, donuts, bagels, and more pastries than you could imagine. Almost all of the block joined in, and Sue smiled to herself in victory for getting all the new neighbors to join. This area is coveted for its quiet streets and optimal shade-to-sun ratio. Most of the residents have been here for thirty-plus years. I was lucky enough to inherit my house from my grandparents. It's rare that anyone new and young moves in, which was why Sara's arrival was such a treat.

I remember the moment I saw her that day.

She's standing with Mr. Vasquez by the coffee station, and I couldn't help but chuckle. This girl wouldn't last five minutes in a casino—she has zero poker face. I could see her boredom from a mile away. To be fair, Mr. Vasquez only has three topics of conversation, and all of them involve his chihuahua.

I make my way over, feigning urgency like I've been summoned.

"Hey," I say, slipping beside Sara, close enough that my arm brushes hers. Electricity zips up my spine at the contact. "There you are. I've been looking everywhere for you."

Her eyes flick to mine, confused for half a second—then something clicks. Relief softens her expression, and she plays along instantly. "Oh—thank God." She sighs, a little breathless. "I mean—yes, here I am."

"Sorry to interrupt." I flash Mr. Vasquez a faux sympathetic smile. "Sue asked me to gather all the new neighbors' contacts. You know how she is." I wink.

Sara nods enthusiastically, clearly desperate to escape this conversation. "Oh yes, I need to get that to her soon so I can be added to the neighborhood watchlist. Wouldn't want anyone taking the packages off my porch."

Mr. Vasquez eyes me suspiciously but doesn't say anything more before he turns to find his next victim. The moment he leaves, Sara exhales like she's been holding her breath for hours.

"You just saved my life," she teases, resting her hand on my forearm for a fraction of a second. "I was three seconds away from faking a phone call."

"Happy to be of service," I reply. "Chihuahua stories are a dangerous sport."

She laughs—really laughs—and something warm settles in my chest.

"Coffee?" I ask, nodding toward the machine.

She tilts her head, studying me, eyes bright. "Only if you promise to never leave me alone with Mr. Vasquez."

"Deal, I'm Dave," I say, giving her hand a firm shake. "You're under my protection now."

Sara and I were inseparable for the rest of the morning. I shared insights about our neighbors with her—okay, we gossiped. I told her about Mr. Bowman and Mrs. Sanders' ongoing feud over the grass height. Or how Sue's cat, Socks— who roams the street during the day—acts as if he's starving. Lastly, I warned her about the HOA's strict policy requiring trash cans be returned from the curb on the same day as pick-up.

We flirted, laughed, and maybe touched a bit more than friendly neighbors should. By the end of *Sunrise on Sundown*, I could tell she was expecting me to ask for her number, but I was too chickenshit to do it. I made up a fake excuse about getting a message from my sister and left before she could even say goodbye. I know—it was a cowardly move.

I set the reusable bags neatly in front of her door—but not close enough that it blocks it from opening—snap a picture for proof, and ring the doorbell. I consider staying and reintroducing myself, but think better of it. There's only so much semi-creepy shit I can do in one day without *actually* being a creep. I already overstepped with the oat milk and astrology questions.

I back away from her house, I make the *incredibly* long thirty-second drive across the street to my own place. As I step onto my porch, I tell myself not to, but I glance back anyway, hoping to catch a glimpse of her, only to find the groceries still untouched on her porch.

2
SARA

An annoyingly cheery, twinkling sound wakes me from sleep. *Damn it.* I fell asleep with my stupid red light mask on again. The slight warmth coming from the *Jason*-esque mask makes me feel like a kitten in a sunbeam.

Being a streamer who's awake all night means keeping up with a very rigorous ten-step Korean skincare routine to make sure I'm not caught looking like a zombie in front of six million people.

Six. Million. It's still absolutely wild to me considering it all started on a whim with my ex-boyfriend—*he who shall not be named*. Now here I am, playing for a global audience *nightly*. Most of them are here for my skills, but the comments on my stream make it pretty obvious that some viewers only stick around for the skimpy outfits and *accidentally* suggestive camera angles. If that's what pays my bills, I'll absolutely exploit the thirst. Within reason, of course.

After last night's extra-late session—and the jump scare I gave myself when I saw the noticeable bags under my eyes, plus my jet-black hair piled into an overly messy topknot—I decided that today I was in need of a little *extra* pampering.

If I swear loyalty to anything in this world, it's sunscreen and snail mucin, but one of my viewers is a dermatology student and suggested adding red-light therapy to my routine three times a week, so that's exactly what I did. After two weeks, I can already see the benefits—my skin is noticeably clearer.

I pull off the mask and blink away the blurriness before grabbing my phone. It's nine in the morning, and I have multiple missed messages. But one important one sticks out.

Your DoorDash order has been delivered.

Please let my oat milk still be safe for consumption.

I shove my blanket off and swing my legs over the edge of the bed, reaching my arms overhead until I feel the relief of my vertebrae stretching. My thin silk cami rides up above my navel, letting a cool breeze brush across my stomach and making me shiver. I shuffle to my reading chair in the corner and grab my plush bathrobe—the one that cost an embarrassing amount of money but was absolutely worth it. If I'm going to be a homebody, I'm going to be a *comfortable* homebody. The robe wraps around me like a teddy bear made exclusively for rich hermits. And technically, that's me.

I make my way to the front door and am pleasantly surprised when I see the bags right outside, but not too close, almost as if the Dasher opened the storm door to make sure it wouldn't block it. With a smile, I grab the reusable bags and shuffle back into my self-proclaimed cave.

Once everything is put away and I've stolen a handful of dry *Frosted Flakes* to munch on, I make a mental note to give Dave a generous tip and rate him five stars for "friendliness." Anyone who takes milk selection that seriously deserves a little extra.

I usually don't talk to anyone outside my social circle, but something about his message made me want to.

It's not that I'm socially closed off; it's that when you hit twenty-five, it's really hard to make friends, and the small talk can be too tedious. Your mid-twenties are not for the weak. One day you're eating your body weight in milkshakes and pizza; the next, you can't even look at a dairy product without needing three Lactaid pills and a prayer.

A wave of exhaustion rolls over me, and I slump against the kitchen counter as I tap the buttons on my coffee machine.

My house isn't what you'd expect from someone making *streamer* money. When I first saw it on the market, the curb appeal immediately drew me in. The small, cottage-style stone build stands apart from the new cookie-cutter houses, and the front porch—with its built-in swing—screams cozy fall evenings. Inside, the home has been upgraded to a more modern standard, with an open layout, oversized windows, and a kitchen that's to die for. It's easily my favorite part of the house. There's a large island with a white marble countertop, a farmhouse sink, a pot-filler faucet mounted to the backsplash, and my absolute favorite feature: the coffee nook built into the cabinetry. The seller called it an *appliance garage*. All I know is that it closes when I'm not making coffee and gives the space a perfectly clean look.

It might be the neat freak in me, but I like having absolutely no clutter in the house. My friend says my place looks like it's on permanent display for potential buyers, but I love it. It's my kingdom.

And the neighborhood is hard to beat. Everyone is so friendly, and they truly take neighborhood watch to another level. One time, my best friend, Sydney, stayed over for the weekend when she was recovering from her LASIK surgery, and Sue from next door immediately called me, claiming 'suspicious activity.' I guess that's what happens when you're a little reclusive; the neighborhood thinks you're some kind of hermit and that a daywalker on your property means an imminent threat.

I drift through the rest of my daily routine: a glass of lemon water, daily vitamins, a freshly brewed latte, checking last night's stream analytics, and decide to film some TikTok clips later.

Settling onto the couch, I'm about to start watching last night's stream highlights, when a notification from DoorDash pops up. It's like my phone is listening to my thoughts.

Rate your delivery.

I give Dave five stars and decide to bump his tip up a few dollars for his dedication to providing me top-tier oat milk. Just as I'm about to close out the app, it asks me a question that stops me in my tracks.

Mark as preferred shopper?

I hover over the button. He was nice, attentive, and easy to talk to—but marking someone as a preferred shopper feels like a big step. I take a sip of my coffee, needing the liquid courage to hit Accept, all while ignoring the small, traitorous voice in my head whispering that I enjoyed talking to him... and maybe —just maybe—want the chance to do it again.

3
SARA

The soft hum of my PC fills the room, providing the white noise I need to drown out the silence between scrolling comments during today's stream. Another message pops up in the chat—something about my outfit.

I try to ignore it, but it lingers like an annoying fly at a Fourth of July picnic.

"If you're going to objectify me, my mods will remove you from the chat," I say into my mic. "I've said it before—I'm here for the game. If you're here for anything else, you can leave."

Normally, comments about my appearance roll right off me. I knew what I signed up for as a female streamer. Objectification, weird DMs, unsolicited opinions—it comes with the territory. Most nights, I'd lean into it, gain a new subscriber, and move on. But tonight, something feels... off. My emotions are muddy, edged with irritation and a prickle of self-consciousness I can't shake.

I glance at my phone and internally scream. Like clockwork. *Shark week.* This is not what I want to deal with today, or any day, really. I swear I suffer from the worst menstrual cramps.

"That's all for tonight, guys. I'm feeling under the weather." I shut down the game as streams of well-wishes fly in from my viewers. Some of them can be so sweet.

Pushing my headset up, I lean back in my chair, stretching until my spine cracks loud enough to echo. A dull ache rolls through my abdomen, the cramps already building in slow, warning waves. My mood teeters on the edge, and I feel like I'm one sentimental TikTok away from dissolving into sobs. My period always hits like a freight train, so I decide to be proactive before it fully derails me.

I open the delivery app and start adding items to my cart. Tampons, ibuprofen, an electric heating pad, and a family-size bag of potato chips. The holy quartet of cycle survival. I toss in a couple of comfort snacks for good measure—because you can never have too many snacks.

After placing the order, I head to my closet and pull on the comfiest outfit known to mankind: leggings and a worn, oversized T-shirt. I finish the look with my bathrobe, tying it loosely for maximum comfort, then make my way into the kitchen for my ultimate menstrual-care comfort ritual.

I fill the kettle with water and set it on the stove. A good cup of tea starts with the right water temperature, and the only way to guarantee that is by boiling it properly on the stovetop. I stand by this statement and will continue to do so until they bury me six feet under.

Fishing a chamomile tea bag from the holder, I drop it into my favorite mug—the one I found perched on top of my mailbox a few months ago. I never figured out who it belonged to, but it was far too cute to toss, so I brought it inside, scrubbed it clean, and kept it safe. I told myself I was performing a public service—rehoming a mug in need. It's white with a red-and-white mushroom cap for a lid, and stamped across the front in cheerful lettering are the words "I'm a fungi."

The kettle begins to whistle, a sharp, impatient sound cutting through the quiet kitchen. I turn off the heat and pour the water slowly, steam rising in soft, curling ribbons. The scent of chamomile blooms almost instantly—warm, floral, faintly sweet—wrapping around me like a hug. I place the mushroom-shaped lid on top, trapping the heat inside as the tea steeps, the mug warming my palms the moment I lift it.

Placing the cup on my designated snack tray, I grab a bag of baking chocolate chips and Chex Mix and add them to the tray before making my way to my couch. After confirming everything is nestled in place on the couch, I collapse back into it and turn on my favorite trashy reality show, *Love Is Blind*. Bring on the drama!

I'm so engrossed in the show that I lose all sense of time—until my cramps start screaming. I reach for the nearly empty bottle of ibuprofen and notice a missed notification on my phone.

My Target order has been delivered. Perfect timing. My uterus is demanding a heating pad. Those disposable ones were not cutting it.

Bless whoever invented delivery apps. I would marry them. Unless they're already married, then I would name my first-born after them. I shuffle to the front door, tightening my robe before opening it to the bite of frigid January air. This is one of the coldest winters we've had in years, and I'm endlessly grateful for whoever braved this weather to shop for me. I'd much rather be warm inside than out there facing the cold.

I freeze when I look down at my doorstep.

Sitting on top of my delivery bags is a plush stuffed animal. Specifically—a brown sloth. I pick it up slowly, fingers sinking into its soft weight, staring into its wide, gentle eyes. Without thinking, I hug it tight against my chest. Something warm melts in my ribs at the small, unexpected kindness. Like the Grinch, I can practically feel my heart grow three sizes.

I glance around the porch and down the quiet street, half-expecting the delivery driver to still be there—even though the order was dropped off two hours ago. Digging through my robe pocket, I try to find my phone. Gosh—darn it. I swear it was right there. The cold air creeps into the house, and I hurry to scoop up the bags and carry them into the kitchen. Once everything is safely inside, I grab the sloth and head back to the couch, still searching.

I find my phone tucked between the cushions. Figures.

Snuggling into the couch with my new bestie, I unlock my phone, navigate to the app, and my jaw nearly drops when I see his name: *Dave.* My oat-milk savior—and now my sloth-bearer.

After contemplating for less than a minute, I add a message—along with a tip.

SARA

Thank you for the sloth. I shall name him Sir Sloths-A-Lot. Seriously. He made my night!

I hit send, my heart racing so hard I can hear it in my ears. I don't know why I'm this nervous over a delivery guy seeing my message... but I hope he does. And a small part of me hopes he'll reply.

4

DAVE

The smell of musk and sweat assaults my senses.

"Alright, we can do this! Three-peat on three," Ravi says, putting his hand in the middle of the group.

"One... two... three-peat!" We cheer before breaking apart and taking our positions.

Three years ago, after a random late-night study session, Ravi saw a sign for the school gym Dodgeball tournament, and he convinced us to sign up. Now, Ravi, Eric, Kyle, Chad, and I have an undefeated record, and this year marks our final year here. We are determined to make it count and leave a lasting legacy in this tournament.

The noise from the opposing team is loud; they're our biggest rivals... The Dental Dudes. Yeah, not the most creative bunch but who's to judge, we named ourselves, The Breathing Bunch.

The sharp whistle from the referee signals the final game of the tournament. It's now or never. I lunge for the line of dodgeballs, managing to snag two before retreating. I toss one towards Kyle, our center. For five guys bonded over the trauma of graduate school, we work as a well-oiled team. Kyle is tall and well-built, with a killer throw. An obvious choice to be our center. Ravi and Eric are smaller in stature but have sharp eyes, and seamlessly transition into our corner positions, catching incoming balls and reviving those who are out. Chad and I fit perfectly in the middle, serving as the runners, the first to grab the balls and ensuring the rear is strong.

Fifteen minutes later, we secure the win.

"YES! I knew we could do it!" Ravi pumps his fist in the air. Out of all of us, he's always the most animated. He takes this tournament very seriously. I tried to sit this year out, but he sent me a PowerPoint explaining why the team needed me and why I needed them. It was quite convincing, especially considering I'm standing here holding this plastic participation trophy.

"Never doubted us," Kyle chimes in from behind me.

"Let's hit the sauna," Chad announces, as he makes his way toward the locker room.

"I'd rather take an ice bath," I counter, feeling my joints start to stiffen.

"And maybe a few beers," Eric interjects.

Ravi wraps his arm around my neck. "That's a great plan. You in, Dave?"

"Probably not," I shake my head, trying to think of a good excuse not to go out. If I told them I'm skipping out on guys' night to pine over a girl, they would never let me live it down.

It's been a week since Sara and I "talked," and since then, I've been lurking in my front yard, hoping to catch her and strike up a casual conversation. I caught a glimpse of her on her porch swing the other day. I'm pretty sure our neighbor, Sue, thinks I've completely lost it—standing outside tending to my yard in the dead of winter.

I was surprised to see her outside in the cold, but I have to admit she looked cozy—adorable, even—all wrapped up in her little cocoon. A small space heater hummed softly at her feet, a blanket draped over her lap. She was wearing one of those oversized blanket hoodies my sister bought for my nephew to keep him warm around the house. A book rested in her hands, and steam curled lazily from the mug beside her.

In my not-so-incognito staring, I recognized that mug—it was *my* mug.

I left it on top of her mailbox weeks ago when I was walking Eliana's dog. They were taking their first vacation with my nephew, and I had reluctantly agreed to dog-sit. Which, in retrospect, was the most disastrous week of my life. My sister had failed to mention that her dog, a Shiba Inu, was still in puppy mode and, at two years old, needed three walks a day. During one of our walks, I got a phone call and between juggling a leash and a ball of excited fur, I didn't want to drop the mug. *It was special.* A Christmas gift from my nephew—something he picked out for me when he was in his weird mushroom obsession phase.

I remember the last delivery I made to Sara—she'd texted me with the funniest commentary about why Target organizes the store like it's trying to test customers' survival skills. I've never had this much fun talking to a girl. Usually, I'm a little reserved and awkward, but something about the way Sara carries herself in conversation makes her easy to talk to. I don't second-guess my messages.

So yeah—I'm going to decline going out for drinks to go home and pretend to casually walk past her house and strike up a conversation.

Maybe today I'll get lucky.

5
DAVE

"Black coffee for Dave," the barista says, sliding a steaming cup of coffee toward the pick-up counter. It's my second cup of the day, and my brain is still in loading mode from memorizing these respiratory drug names for my upcoming exam. Seriously, does the person who names these drugs get a bonus at their company? Why are they so hard to pronounce? *And* spell? Sounding it out doesn't even help.

Even though I want to pull my hair out every other day, I'm thankful that I was accepted into the respiratory therapy program. When my grandpa—who we call Zayde—was diagnosed with lung cancer when I was twenty, we all thought that was the end. But he was resilient; he didn't let the cancer take him down. He responded to treatment, and although he got sick more often, he was a fighter.

During the last two years of his life, he was in and out of the hospital often with respiratory illnesses. If it wasn't pneumonia, it was his chronic obstructive pulmonary disease, or *COPD*, acting up. The respiratory therapists at the hospital were the reason I decided to go into this program. It wasn't only a way to honor my Zayde, but also to help someone else's version of Zayde.

I'm thankful my time has been preoccupied with rotations and exams since all my spare time keeps reverting back to Sara, and I'm starting to think she blocked me on her DoorDash app. How do I know? Well, call it being a good neighbor and not a stalker. And technically, I was on neighborhood watch duty for a week, per Sue. Which means it was totally valid that I checked in to see deliveries at her doorstep.

I'm walking back toward my corner of the coffee shop, which I've commandeered since they opened at seven this morning, when my phone buzzes. As if the universe heard me thinking about her, a DoorDash delivery request pops up—from *her*.

I accept the request and scan her list for today. Flu medicine, can of chicken noodle soup, crackers, and electrolyte drinks.

My brain screams: *She's sick. She needs me.*

Without a second thought, I know exactly what I need to do. With a short window before I get dinged for not delivering on time, I pack up my bags and head home.

Thirty minutes later, the smell of chicken and herbs floats through my kitchen, reminding me of time with my grandmother, Bubbe. She used to make me chicken soup with matzo balls whenever I was under the weather. When Zayde's vision worsened, and he was no longer able to drive her to the market, I would make grocery trips with her, and we would come home to cook all kinds of dishes. Anytime I cook her recipes, it's like she's standing right next to me, guiding me.

Ladling soup and matzo balls into a container, I set it aside to cool while I gather all the other items necessary for her recovery. Using an old picnic basket I have stored in the garage, I pack it with the flu medicines, tissues, cough drops, Tylenol and a six-pack of BODYARMOR.

The soup isn't part of her order. It's definitely past *border-line* overstepping, but I can picture her opening the basket, finding it, and smiling. And something about being the person who puts a smile on her face causes me to throw caution to the wind.

Honestly, she might report me.

But fuck it.

I open the delivery app. I see I have ten minutes left before I'm due to deliver. I hit the "cancel order" button and pray this time she really won't call the police on me.

6

SARA

I. AM. DYING.

This is what death must feel like. My body is heavy and weightless at the same time, like gravity can't decide what to do with me. Every movement sends tingles down my limbs, and my head spins if I so much as *blink*. I curl tighter into my blanket nest, hugging Sir Sloths-A-Lot, and groan into the pillow.

I can't remember the last time I was sick; it feels like an eternity. When your job and social life are in the comfort of the four walls in your house, you really don't have a chance to share germs with others. Yet here I am, on my deathbed. Okay, that might be an exaggeration, but right now, if Ed McMahon came in offering me a million dollars to get up and do the chicken dance, I would not be on the receiving end of one of his big checks.

I'm drifting off to sleep when my phone rings with a familiar tone. The sound of Saweetie's *"Best Friend"* comes through my phone, signaling the only person I would pick up calls from.

"Hey, Sydney," I manage to squeak out.

"Oh, honey, you sound miserable."

"Geez, thanks." My voice drips with sarcasm.

"I was calling to check on you before my flight to Portland." The sound of a flight attendant telling everyone to switch their phone to airplane mode comes through the line. "I didn't know if I should call the local police station for a wellness check." She teases me, but I can sense a hint of concern in her voice.

Sydney—my best friend for life—my ride or die. If I ever needed to bury a body, I would call her before my brother, Owen. When my family first moved to Eagleton, when I was eight, she was the first friend I made. We were inseparable growing up, always spending time at each other's houses. When I got my period, Sydney was the first one I called. When she kissed her first boyfriend, we stayed up until midnight discussing the event. Over time, she became more like a sister to me than a friend.

"I feel like death, and I blame you." I sniffle, sounding like Sneezy from Snow White.

"Me?" She whisper-shouts, no doubt she's already in trouble for still having her phone out while the plane is about to take off.

"Yes, you're the only one I've been in close physical contact with." I readjust to a more comfortable position, and my head stages a full riot. "Did you maybe pick it up from Xander? Is it confirmed to be the flu? What does he have?"

"I'm so sorry, sweetie. I wish I could tell you," she says apologetically. "But I'm not seeing Xander anymore."

"Oh, I didn't know. I'm sorry."

"It's fine—he just wasn't a fit." Her voice softens. "Now, tell me, is there anything you need before my flight takes off?"

"No, I should be okay. I put in a DoorDash order for some soup. Hopefully, it gets here soon."

"Sara—canned soup? Why didn't you get fresh soup delivered?"

"I crave chicken noodle soup, and the canned version always provides comfort." I grab another cough drop from the bag, popping it in my mouth and depositing the wrapper in my growing mountain of used tissues.

"Hmm, does it? Or does the idea of talking to a certain delivery guy soothe you?" She teases. I regret letting her know about the flirtatious conversations Dave and I have been having. She's been pressuring me to ask for his real number. I know she means well, but it's too much right now for me.

"It's not that—you know I'm not ready to jump into another relationship."

She scoffs lightly. "Sara, it's been five years. You need to give yourself a chance again."

"I know, maybe soon." I slump into my blankets, finding comfort in the warmth of my bed. "Hey, I'm starting to get sleepy again, I'll talk to you soon?" I say, wanting to end this conversation about me and any potential guy.

"Okay, I'll check on you once I'm in Portland. Love you."

"Love you, too." I hang up the phone and curl back into bed, drifting in and out of consciousness.

The next time I wake up, it's from the buzzing of my phone. There was a buzz at my doorbell. I open my phone to check who it could be when I see a DoorDash notification with a cancellation to my order. *Great.* I'm already feeling like shit and now I can't even get my damn soup.

I drag myself out of bed for another cup of tea and to investigate the front door. When I open it, I'm greeted by a brown, wicker picnic basket. That's odd. Who would be going on a picnic in this cold season? I look around the porch, I try to see if the person who left it was still around. Seeing no one, I grab the basket and take it inside.

Please be empty. This isn't the fire station. I'm not mentally equipped for that story line.

I place it on the kitchen island and look inside. The first thing I see is a handwritten note:

> You deserve better than canned soup when you're sick.
> I hope you enjoy it, it's a family recipe.
>
> —Dave

Inside the basket is a container of soup that smells like heaven. It's hot too, super hot—like it just came off the stove. Along with flu medicines, tissues, cough drops, Tylenol, and six bottles of BODYARMOR.

If my body wasn't already achy from being sick, I would be a puddle on the floor. I can't believe he made me home-made soup—and I have no way of telling him thank you.

7
SARA

It's been two weeks since the soup delivery, and every time I look at my sloth, I'm reminded of Dave's gentle gestures. The way he took care of me when I was sick. Sir Sloths-A-Lot has become my emotional support buddy. He's on my lap when I'm gaming or on the couch binge-watching trashy reality TV. I even bring him to bed with me every night. I keep getting the urge to text Dave, but don't know how to reach him other than through a DoorDash order.

A small part of me feels ridiculous for obsessing over someone I barely know, especially someone I've only ever interacted with through text messages and grocery bags. I don't even know what he looks like.

I've checked my front-door cam more times than I'd like to admit, trying to get a sense of what he looks like. Unfortunately, I haven't been able to see his face. I've only caught glimpses of his hands and shoulders when he's delivered my order. And yet... there's a pull I can't explain.

On the last delivery, I was able to make out the shape of his face, a bit with the moonlight illuminating a defined jaw. He looks shorter than my brother Owen—maybe five-eight at best. It's hard to tell through the camera with the way my house is situated; the driveway is one the side, so I can barely make out the color of the car, let alone the model. If I had that information, I could hand it over to Sydney to investigate. That girl has the detective skills of a CIA agent. I bet she could figure out his name, birthday, and mother's maiden name in less than fifteen minutes.

I really should get out more often. Maybe Sydney and I can go out this weekend; it's time to get back out there. Especially if I'm trying to use DoorDash like a dating app. This hermit-style living doesn't bode well for my sex life. My battery-operated boyfriend (BoB) practically lives on the charger nowadays. I reach for my phone, shooting off a text to Sydney while getting my snacks ready for tonight's stream.

SARA

I'm thinking about going out this weekend.

SYDNEY

I'm calling the authorities because who are you and what have you done with my best friend?

SARA

Don't be dramatic. I just think it's time to get back out there, meet a guy, possibly, retire BoB, you know?

SYDNEY

Yesss! Girl, I have been saying you need to get out there. It's been approximately three fiscal years since you've touched another human voluntarily.

SARA

That's not true. I held the barista's hand that one time.

SYDNEY

You held his hand because he was having a panic attack over a bad joke you made about being allergic to dairy.

He thought he was killing you.

SARA

To be fair, technically, if I have dairy, it does kill me a little. Those twenty minutes on the toilet are like death.

SYDNEY

Okayyyyy, we're getting off topic. To summarize, touching a barista doesn't count; we need a real man.

One that pushes you against a door and dusts off the cobwebs, if you know what I mean.

SARA

Yes, I know what you mean.

SYDNEY

Perfect! What are we wearing?

SARA

Something that says "approachable but mysterious." But also "will leave by ten."

SYDNEY

Wrong. You're wearing something that says "I look like a good girl, but I'll be your good little slut."

SARA

I regret texting you.

SYDNEY

No, you don't. You love me because I'm right.

We're not leaving the bars until you're going home with someone or you get a quickie in the bathroom stall.

SARA

Those are some high-ticket items.

SYDNEY

I will make sure it happens; those cobwebs are trembling.

SARA

Alright, alright, I know you're right. I'll meet you Saturday at Eagleton Saloon around seven.

SYDNEY

Sounds great. Love you!

SARA

I love you too. Thanks, Syd.

SYDNEY

Anytime, babe.

I pocket my phone and pull out rice, tuna, and seaweed wraps—perfect little late-night snacks. Easy to grab, easy to eat between sessions.

As I make my way back to my computer, I spot Sir Sloths-A-Lot waiting in my chair, and my thoughts drift—inevitably—back to Dave. To the quiet thoughtfulness behind his purchases.

The urge to place another order, just to talk to him again, hits so hard I can't deny it anymore.

I grab my phone and open the DoorDash app before the logical side of my brain can talk me out of it. My fingers hover over the screen as I scroll through the grocery lists I had preselected; my heartbeat is unusually fast. It's like playing Russian roulette, but with my DoorDash shopper.

I fill the cart, add the essentials, and then I pause, staring at the "Submit Order" button. My palms are sweaty as I hover my thumb over the screen. I can't help the nervous excitement buzzing in my chest.

Come on, Dave. Be my shopper. *Please.*

8

DAVE

I'm halfway down the frozen food aisle when my phone buzzes.

At first, I think it's a notification from my study group—another flashcard reminder, or "don't forget the midterm" nudge, but no. It's the DoorDash app, a new delivery request from Sara. It's been two weeks since I delivered her groceries, and with each delivery, our flirtation has grown a little bolder. Each time, I'm tempted to reveal it's me, but I hold back. What if she doesn't feel the same? What if she doesn't remember me? What if she thinks I'm creepy?

Those thoughts plague me every time I see her around. I tried to approach her a few times, but Sue kept getting in the way. *Seriously, how many HOA updates can we have in a month?* So here I am, using a damn delivery app for dating—if you can even call it dating.

Our last text exchange plays on loop in my head every night.

SARA

Did you know Corn Flakes were eaten by astronauts on the Apollo 11 moon landing?

DAVE

Oh, really? So you're saying if I want to be an astronaut, I should eat Corn Flakes for training?

SARA

Precisely! It's obviously the far superior cereal since it has been in space. No other cereal compares.

DAVE

Is that why you have me picking up two boxes this week?

SARA

No, I'm having you pick up two because I want you to keep one. Think of me when you're eating it.

I know I will when I'm enjoying it… late at night

I shake my head, refocusing on the order in front of me, and shove my feelings and attractions away. That's a problem for future Dave.

I accept the order, then rearrange my current order for Gretchen. I don't want to mix up their order or miss picking up a requested item. This job may be my side gig, but I pride myself in my work; I've never gotten a complaint for a wrong delivery. My phone buzzes in the cart with a message from Sara.

SARA

Thanks for taking my order again. You must really like Target.

I grin like an idiot, my fingers flying over the screen.

DAVE

Only because I think you're worth the extra aisle-cruising.

A little digital ping tells me she's read it. My chest tightens in a way I can't explain. Flirting with her is so easy, even when I'm being a complete goofball.

I finish loading her items into my cart, double-check to make sure I got everything, then make my way to the check-out. It was a small order today, and nothing that was super urgent. It makes me wonder if she requested another delivery just to talk to me. The thought has me excited at the possibility of more. Maybe today, I should wait at her door during drop-off and tell her who I really am.

I'm loading the last bag into my trunk when a message from Aiden comes through.

AIDEN

Hey! Do you have plans tonight?

DAVE

Nothing solid planned. What's up? Need me to watch Jake again?

Aiden is my neighbor, a few houses down. He and his best friend, Eli, moved in a few months after Sara.

Mr. Jones finally decided it was time to retire to Florida—said he was done with the unpredictable weather—and put his house on the market. Since the housing market was down at the time, the place went fast. I think it took them less than a week to close and move in.

I've puppy-sat for Aiden a few times while he was in the middle of his medical internship, and now I usually do it whenever he and his girlfriend, Charlie, go out of town. She's the sweetest. Every time I watch Jake—their Yorkie mix—she brings over a loaf of homemade sourdough as a thank-you. It usually lasts about two days before I'm dragging myself to the gym with Eli on day three, trying to work off the extra carbs.

Funny story—Eli is dating Charlie's twin sister, Claire. And Aiden and Charlie actually got together after he mistook Charlie for Claire during a fake kidnapping he and Eli planned. I know—it's one of those stories that sounds so far-fetched it could be a movie plot. I remember when they first told me at Eagleton Saloon, I was convinced they were messing with me.

AIDEN

Not this weekend. Charlie took him back to Everly Falls.

I swear she loves that dog more than she loves me.

Eli and I were going to grab a beer at Eagleton Saloon, just seeing if you wanted to join.

DAVE

Oh yeah, man. I'll be there.

I could use the distraction from thinking about Sara. Especially since she's been consuming my late-night thoughts more often than she should.

9
SARA

"Damnnnn, girl, you're getting laid tonight," Sydney says as she breezes through my front door.

She oozes confidence, dressed in a black leather skirt, black turtleneck sweater, and black combat boots. Her braids are tied up in a bun, with a few strands hanging loose, framing her face. Her smoky eyes and cat-eye liner are sharp enough to cut glass, and she smells faintly of vanilla and bad decisions.

"Thanks," I say, swiping gloss over my red lipstick.

I steal a quick glance at the hallway mirror and, honestly, I'm impressed. I cleaned up well. I'm wearing a black lace bodysuit that accentuates my chest, the bodice hugging my curves and giving me a perfect hourglass shape. I pair it with black jeans and black heeled ankle booties. The outfit might not be warm, but it makes a statement.

And that statement is: I'm single and ready to mingle.

"Alright, let's get out there and clean these webs." Sydney says, dragging me out the door. Grabbing my leather coat, I roll my eyes at her commitment to this cobwebs joke.

The smell of sweat, perfume, and cheap beer hangs thick in the air as we walk into Eagleton Saloon. I might make good money from streaming, but it's hard to pass up the classic college-town experience of a grimy local dive bar. Ever since streaming became my main source of income, going to college for a degree I'd probably never use felt like a waste of money. That didn't stop me from soaking up the full college-party experience, though—especially with Sydney as my wing woman.

Before my streaming career took off, we went out a lot more often. Not that I liked going out often—it was more because I like hanging out with Sydney. Sydney is an absolute knockout—the real-life embodiment of Samantha from *Sex and the City*. She's unapologetically herself—true to her wants, needs, and desires. The world would be a better place if we were all a little more like her.

"I'm going to go realign my crystals," Sydney shouts, already digging through her purse. "The energy in that Uber was absolutely not the vibe."

She pulls out a small velvet pouch like she's about to perform a ritual. She gives me a pointed look. "Do not leave. Do not hide in the bathroom. I'll be back in five." Then she disappears into the crowd, crystals in hand.

Over the next ten minutes, I'm reminded of why I stopped going out with Sydney. In the short span of time, I've been bumped into by a drunk sorority girl trying to find her friends, and two frat bros almost turn me into a sandwich, and *not* the fun kind. The kind that reminds me that standing at five-foot nothing *sucks,* and *far* too many of these men are rocking sweat stains in very unflattering areas. A part of me wants to call an Uber, go back home, and snuggle on the couch with Sir Sloths-A-Lot, but Sydney's words echo in my head.

Dust off the cobwebs.

Finally, I find a small pocket of space at the bar and wedge myself in, waiting for the bartender to spot me. I guess being short does have *some* advantages. The bartender looks up, eyes flicking over me with open appreciation. He lingers just a tad too long on my breasts before meeting my eyes. He looks to be about my age, twenty-five, and definitely gives off the vibes that he would entertain the idea of going home with one of the women from the bar...I'll keep him as a backup for my cobwebs.

"What can I get you?" he asks, voice smooth, eyes clear with mischief, and leaning in a little too close for my liking.

"Vodka soda," I reply, matching his tone. He's definitely easy on the eyes. Sharp jawline, dark green eyes, a little five o'clock shadow, and a smile that definitely gets him good tips with the ladies.

"You come here often?" He slides my glass to me, our fingers grazing, but I don't get any fuzzy feelings.

"Sometimes." That earns a laugh. Before he can continue his flirtatious endeavors, his coworker cuts him off, pointing to the needy customers at the end of the bar.

I scan the room slowly, letting my gaze drift over clusters of people pressed shoulder to shoulder, laughter spilling over the music. I'm not desperate—just... open. Curious. Tonight feels like a night meant for possibility.

That's when I lock eyes with Eli. Another resident of Sundown Court.

He's posted up near the high-top tables with his roommate, Aiden, both of them nursing beers.

I know Aiden and Eli mostly by proximity—neighbors a few houses down who both moved in a few weeks after me. I never really talked to them until recently, when Jake—Aiden's puppy—followed me home one day. I guess Aiden's been training him to protect his girlfriend, Charlie, and I must have looked similar because Jake followed me. I'm glad he did, though, because Charlie came by to get him, and I found out she's the brilliant mind behind my favorite local-ish bakery. It's located in Everly Falls, about two hours away, but I was so addicted to their sourdough fudge brownies that I'd have paid for overnight shipping. Now that I've met Charlie, she actually hand-delivers them whenever she comes into town, and it's the best thing ever.

Eli grins when he spots me and lifts his chin in greeting, curling two fingers in a casual *come-hither* motion. I smile back, already weaving through the crowd toward them.

And then I see him—*Dave*. The neighbor I've been playing what-ifs in my brain for the last five years.

He's standing a little off to the side, half-turned toward the bar like he's observing, more than participating. Recognition hits me all at once, pulling me backward in time.

The breakfast block party—*Sunrise on Sundown*. After he rescued me from Mr. Vasquez, we hit it off, or at least I *thought* we did. I figured he would have asked for my number, but he never did. It was a blow to my self-esteem, especially since I was coming off of a breakup. But time went by, and I only saw him casually, from time to time. We never really had another opportunity. Maybe tonight is the night.

My gaze drifts back to him, taking him in properly this time. He looks like he walked out of a GQ shoot in his navy boyfriend sweater and khakis. He seems taller—*broader* —than the first time we met. I wonder if it's because he's hanging out with Aiden and Eli. It seems like he's taken on their physique, and considering they're both ex-Marines, it's not a bad one to take after. His short brown hair sits neatly on his head, making me want to run my hands through it and mess it up. Soft, honey-brown eyes meet my gaze, and the smallest hint of a smile brightens his face.

I slide into the space beside Aiden, Eli nodding in greeting.

"Hey, what are you guys up to tonight?" I ask, taking a sip of my drink and pretending not to notice Dave moving closer at my side.

"Not much. Trying to decompress after the code we both

had today in the hospital," Eli replies. Aiden gives me a half-hearted grunt.

"How's Charlie?" I ask, knowing Aiden will rarely pass up an opportunity to talk about his girlfriend.

As predicted, I'm greeted by a rare Aiden smile as he talks about her.

"She's good. Her bakery is set to open at the end of the year." Aiden's eyes soften as he talks about her. I wish I could find someone who adores me as much as Aiden adores Charlie.

"That's awesome! I'll have to make a trip with Sydney to see the place."

I catch Dave watching me, and for a moment, the noise of the bar fades away. His mouth curves into a slow smile, like he's been debating whether to come say hi.

10
DAVE

Here she is.

    Sara.

I feel like a teenager trying to figure out if his crush likes him—not a twenty-seven-year-old man—who really should have his hormones together. She looks absolutely breathtaking tonight. The bodice of her lace top hugs her curves, catching the light just enough to draw my eye without begging for it. Black jeans. Heeled ankle boots.

"Hi," I say first, because if I don't, I might lose my nerve.

"Hi," she says, smiling, and for a second I forget how to breathe.

"You come here often?" I tease, and to my surprise, she chortles. A chuckle and snort rolled into one—and coming from her, it's downright adorable.

"I'm sorry," she mumbles, trying to catch her breath. "The bartender used the same line on me less than five minutes ago."

Rubbing a hand behind my neck, I feel my face heat ten degrees. "Oh. Well, I guess we all get tongue-tied around beautiful women."

This time, it's her face that heats. "Smooth."

"Really, though, I've never seen you here before."

"I'm usually busy at night." She takes a sip of her drink, and I watch as her tongue slides over her bottom lip. "I'm a League of Legends streamer, so most of my nights are locked into the computer."

"I see." The reason for her late-night grocery orders comes into focus. "I guess you must be pretty popular?"

"More or less." She looks anywhere but at me, fidgeting with the napkin on the table. Interesting—so she's shy about her streaming.

Clearing my throat, I set my beer down on the table. "I'd love to watch one of your sessions."

"You play?"

I shake my head. "Not to the level of streamers, but I dabble in Black Ops here and there."

"Hmmm," she hums, seeming to be deep in thought.

Not wanting this to turn awkward, I decide to get out of my comfort zone.

"Do you want to dance?" I ask, my hand outstretched for what feels like an eternity.

Her eyes light up, and she gives me a small nod, placing her hand in mine. "Let's do it."

My palm settles on her waist as soon as we hit the dance floor. Her body is warm under my touch. The music turns from upbeat to a slower, more seductive beat. The kind that invites closeness. We move together easily. Instinctively—like we've done this before, in another life.

Her hands rest on my shoulders as I rock us to the beat. The crowd fades until it's just us, swaying together, breathing the same air. She tilts her head back slightly, looking up at me with her deep, onyx eyes, and suddenly my feet feel like they're made of lead. I'm locked in place, captivated by her.

My eyes drop to her lips. The space between us shrinks.

Is this real?

Is this *actually* happening?

My heart pounds in my chest, shock and want tangling together in a heady combination that's clouding every thought. The attraction between us is palpable.

I drop my forehead to hers, a silent question passing between us. When she doesn't move, I lean in, slow and careful, giving her the chance to pull away.

She doesn't.

Instead, she rises up just enough to meet me halfway, her breath hitching as our noses brush. My hand tightens at her waist at the same time she curls her hands into my shirt.

But just before our lips touch, a shrill voice comes from behind Sara, breaking our bubble.

"Sara! Oh my god, there you are!" A woman materializes out of nowhere, looping an arm through Sara's like she's claiming her prize. "I've been looking everywhere for you." When she looks over and notices me standing across from them, her eyes widen. "Oh, I'm sorry. Did I interrupt?"

Sara plasters on a polite smile. "Just a little." She rolls her eyes, but there's no malice to it. And no annoyance in her tone. They must be close.

"I knew you had taste, but damn."

"Sydney," Sara groans.

"You're welcome, by the way," Sydney says to me as she gestures up and down Sara's body. "Her outfit was entirely influenced by yours truly."

Sydney must see the heat in my eyes, so she whispers something to Sara that makes her eyes snap to mine and her cheeks pinken.

"Alright, I'll leave you to it." And just like that, Sydney disappears into the crowd.

Sara rolls her lips together and then chuckles lightly. "Do you want a drink?"

"Yeah." I laugh. "I could use one."

We claim a quiet corner of the bar, half-hidden from the chaos. The music is still loud, but back here it's muted, like the world decided to give us a little pocket of peace, and we talk.

About nothing. About *everything*.

I found out the woman who interrupted us was her best friend, Sydney. She has one brother. She loves streaming, but it can be exhausting to be watched all the time. I tell her about my sister, my nephew, my classes—careful not to reveal my side hustle.

We discover we both like quiet mornings and comfort routines, and that words of affirmation is her love language while mine is something called acts of service. We both secretly judge people who hate naps. We both collect small, sentimental things we pretend aren't sentimental.

I find myself laughing more tonight than I have in months. And it's all because of her.

11

SARA

"Do you want to come back to my place?" I ask, the words leaving my mouth before I can second-guess them.

His eyebrows lift, surprise flickering across his face—then something darker. Heavier.

Want. Clear and unmistakable.

"Yeah," he says, voice low. "I really do."

Our Uber driver, Steve—according to the in-app bio—is a Middle Eastern man in his late fifties, who looks like he'd invite you in for a cup of chai, cookies, and send you home with fruit from his garden. He definitely takes this job very seriously, offering us cold water bottles and even letting us pick the playlist. Music is the last thing on my mind though. All I've been able to think about was the almost kiss on the dance floor, the way his arm held me, and the look in his eyes—like I was something precious to him.

The bar is only a few blocks from our houses, which should take ten to fifteen minutes, if there's no traffic.

I can be patient.

I can keep my hormones in check.

At least that's what I tell myself—until I catch Dave checking me out.

Even in the dark backseat, I can feel his heated gaze on me. Each lingering stare tightens something low in my belly, my body pulled taut like a bowstring, trembling with anticipation.

His knee brushing mine with every turn feels like a slow tease of what's to come. My fingers toy with the edge of his jacket sleeve, testing the boundary. He watches me do it, jaw tight, eyes flicking down and back up again. When his hand finally settles on my thigh, I lean into him, my head resting on his shoulder.

I don't know if it's the vodka, or the proximity of Dave, but I'm feeling warm. I'm normally not this bold, and definitely not an exhibitionist, so I know it's entirely fueled by the liquid courage running through my veins, but all I want to do right now is shove his pants down and have him take me right here in the back of this Uber.

Smiling at him, I lean in, tilting my chin up and letting our lips meet. The kiss is gentle, almost hesitant, like neither of us wants to break the spell we're currently under. His lips feather over mine, soft and tender, sending the little butterflies in my stomach into flight.

The car lurches forward, a panicked "*sorry*" said from the driver's seat making us both laugh.

Dave leans in again, capturing my lips a second time, and this kiss is more urgent, more seeking, as his tongue explores mine. His mouth moves against mine in perfect, calculated movements, like he's trying to memorize every second. The pace is punishingly slow and makes me want to crawl into his lap and make myself a permanent resident.

Without second-guessing, that's exactly what I do.

Dave doesn't stop kissing me as I settle into his lap, swinging both arms around his neck to pull him closer. He matches my eagerness with his own, nibbling on my bottom lip. I can't help the involuntary moan that escapes. The hand supporting my back moves to my hair—he guides me to exactly where he wants me, and the possessiveness in his touch and kiss is making me feral.

"Dave." My voice is barely audible; the need coursing through me has me grinding my ass into his hard length, causing him to break our kiss.

"Baby," he groans into my ear, the warmth of his breath sending goosebumps racing along my arm. His voice drops, rough and barely restrained. "If you don't stop, it's going to be very embarrassing when I get out of this car."

The word *"baby"* does something to me. It warms me from the inside out—and at the same time, it makes me want to show him just how good I can make him feel.

I double down, pressing kisses along his neck, lingering there before repeating the motion just behind his ear. When I feel the subtle twitch beneath me, satisfaction curls low in my stomach. His hands tighten on my waist, the pressure almost bruising, possessive—and I love every second of it.

"God, I really hope you know how to use that thing." I whisper in his ear. "I have plans for you."

He growls—literally—into my neck just as the car reaches my house.

"We're here!" Steve sings-songs from the driver's seat, oblivious to what's been going on in the back seat of his car.

12

DAVE

We've barely cleared the threshold of her door before I'm burying my face in her neck, breathing in her intoxicating scent of vanilla with a hint of florals. I can't think straight; the blood is rushing toward the wrong head as I guide her backward toward the couch. The only coherent thought left is the need to taste her. *Now.*

"Baby," I murmur between kisses. "I need to—"

Sara cuts me off, pushing me down onto the cushions before settling over me. My hands move instinctively, gripping her ass. God, she has a perfect ass—round, soft, tempting enough to make me want to sink my teeth into it.

Later, I tell myself.

If I can hold out that long.

"Sara, baby," I manage. The way her tongue is exploring me is making it nearly impossible to think. Still, I force the words out. "I need to taste you." My voice edged with desperation. "Please. Can I?"

Her pupils are blown wide, her gaze glazed and dark.

"Taste me?" she repeats, brow furrowing slightly, like the

idea is brand new. "No one has ever wanted to…" she whispers.

"Are you telling me," I ask quietly, reverently, "that I'd be the first man between these gorgeous thighs of yours?"

Her nod is barely there, hesitant—but it's enough. And the realization lights something fierce and possessive in my chest as I revel in the fact that I might be her first.

"Fuck, baby," I growl as I flip her over, so she's pinned beneath me. How can this gorgeous, independent, successful woman have never had her pussy eaten before? "You deserve to be worshiped, Sara. And I'll get on my knees for you every day if you'll let me." I pepper soft kisses along her jaw and down her neck, loving how her breath hitches when I reach the top of her breast.

Sitting back on my heels, I admire her sprawled out for me, her chest rising and falling as I take in the sight before me. Her raven hair is fanned out beneath her like a crown, and her perky breasts are on full display in her lace top, the curve of her hourglass frame evident beneath her black jeans.

"I need you," she pleads.

My hands caress her sides until I reach my desired destination, grabbing a handful of each breast. I knead them, my fingers rubbing circles through the lace, until she's writhing under me. Tugging the lace down, they spring free, and I lower myself to her left nipple, sucking and nibbling, taking note of the way her body reacts and savoring each sound she makes so I can do it again, next time.

"My top is a bodysuit," she pants, as I swirl my tongue around the swollen bud of her nipple.

"A bodysuit? Like *Iron Man*?"

That earns me a chuckle. "No—there's a set of buttons at the bottom, so I need to take off my jeans to remove it."

"Are you offering me a strip tease, baby?"

The coy smile she gives me tells me that's *exactly* what I am getting.

I move off of her, settling back into the corner of her sectional, my arms draped across the back like I have all the time in the world.

She reaches for the remote on her coffee table to turn on some music. I track her movements as she saunters back towards me. Something catches my eye—the sloth I got her. Guilt over not telling her I'm the same guy that's been flirting with her on a delivery app sinks between my ribs. But then she unbuttons her jeans and is shimmying out of them, bending over with her ass right at my eye level and the guilt turns into want.

She pops the snaps on the bodysuit, pulls it off over her head, and saunters towards me in nothing but a red lace thong that matches the color of her painted lips. Images of her on her knees, my hands in her hair, and those fucking red lips wrapped around my cock have me harder than a rock. But I meant what I said, and I plan to worship her sweet pussy as long as she'll let me.

Once she's within reach, I pull her onto the couch, switching our positions so I can even the playing field. I stand, and she comes face-to-face with my aching cock. Her eyes are hungry as she takes me in. I make a swift move to strip down to my boxers and hastily rip my shirt over my head.

Sara eyes me hungrily. I preen under her gaze as she takes me in. Then I drop to my knees, using my shoulder to spread her legs and keep them where I want them.

I trail my lips up her legs, nipping at the soft skin of her inner thighs, building her anticipation. My hand glides over her stomach—*is that a belly ring? Holy hell. This girl will be the death of me.* Sara squirms, breathy little pants leaving her mouth as I get closer to her pussy.

"How much would you hate me if I ripped these off of you?" I ask, hooking my finger into the red lace.

Her mouth drops open before she tucks her bottom lip between her teeth and shakes her head. "Not at all."

My cock throbs violently against the couch cushion, and I smirk, pressing a kiss to her covered core, before tugging the lace until it shreds. "Good answer."

I don't waste a moment before diving in.

"Oh my God," she gasps when my tongue makes contact with her clit. Her fingers dig into my scalp while she grips my hair, and I relish in the slight sting.

I curl my hands over her thighs, holding her tightly against me, as I continue to lap at her slit until I feel her thighs trembling around my head. She's close. I start sucking harder, the taste of her on my tongue making my cock twitch in my boxers. He's eager to come out and play, but I can't stop what I'm doing. I'm dizzy with desperation, high on the idea that I'm the first man to make her come undone with just my mouth.

13
SARA

My body feels like it's on fire. I don't think I've ever been this turned on in my life.

The sight of him kneeling in front of me sends a different emotion coursing through me. I finally understand what all the female characters in the books I read are saying.

It's intoxicating to know this man is submitting to me. I have *never* felt so powerful.

Dave definitely knows what he's doing; as his tongue and mouth expertly play with my clit. He's alternating between licks and kisses and my brain is having a hard time keeping up. It's like the motherboard is still loading while all the hard drives are trying to boot up at once.

Every time I feel close to tipping over the edge, he slows his pace, drawing it out and building me back up. For a split second, an irrational part of me is jealous of the women before me. But the red haze of jealousy is replaced with lust when he swipes a finger up my core and pinches my clit.

"Oh." My lips part, my body nearly convulsing off the couch from the sensation.

"Too much?" His voice is full of concern.

"No... it was just... different."

"Must be a good different, 'cause you're soaked, baby." He teases his finger at my entrance. "Do you need me to fill up this needy little pussy?" Dave asks before gliding his tongue over my sensitive core. He hovers just above where I need him, and the combination of his hot breath and hand kneading my thighs have me squirming underneath his touch.

"Yes," I practically pant.

"Hmm, I like hearing you need me. But we need to get you ready first." He pushes one digit in. "God, baby, you're so tight. I can't wait to feel this sweet pussy wrapped around my cock."

"Please." Fuck, I need him. *Now.*

"Not yet," he says as he focuses back on my clit, sucking, tasting, teasing. "First, I need you to come all over my tongue."

He adds another digit, fingers curling, coaxing the next moans out of me. Before I know it, my whole body spasms and I'm coming from oral for the first time. Dave emerges from between my legs; the sight of him wiping his mouth with the back of his hand has me feeling bold.

I push myself up from the couch, grab his hand, and lead him towards my bedroom. I'm completely naked while he's still in his boxers.

"Lose the boxers," I command.

He slides out of his boxers, cock springing free. I watch as he wraps a hand around his hardening length and strokes it from base to tip.

"What's next, baby?" He asks, his voice low and seductive.

"Now, it's my turn to taste you," I answer before pushing him back onto the bed.

I take my time crawling up towards him, loving the way his eyes darken as I approach. Wrapping my lips around his hard shaft, I swirl my tongue at the tip before taking him all the way to the back of my throat.

"Holy hell," he murmurs huskily. "Just like that, baby. I like it like that." I love hearing how good I'm making him feel. Maybe I have a praise kink. That's something to explore.

Right now, all I can think about is the sound he's making and how much I'm enjoying knowing that I'm the one in control of his pleasure. My eyes start to water as I take him deep.

"I'm not going to last like this," he pants. "Those fucking red lips." Before I have time to react, his arms hook underneath me, pulling me up towards his mouth. I can still taste myself on his lips, and the thought has me grinding on his cock.

"Condoms?" he grits out.

I nod toward my nightstand, and he immediately pushes off the bed, moving with an easy confidence that makes my breath hitch. I take a greedy look at him as he turns, the lines of his body catching the light—broad shoulders, a narrow waist, dark ink stretching across his chest, tattoos usually hidden giving him the neighbor-next-door vibe. But now, in the soft glow of my bedroom, Dave is definitely anything but the neighbor next door.

Who knew Dave was *this* hot?

He looks over, catching my gaze, as if he can hear my thoughts. Heat creeps up my neck as I look away, pretending my reaction isn't written all over my face, even as my heart starts racing with anticipation.

"Like what you see?" he says, tearing the wrapper with his teeth—so hot—I can feel my body aching for another release. I watch as he rolls the condom on, and crawls his way up the bed towards me. He's like a lion, slowly stalking his prey and I am a willing offering.

I feel his firm hands grip my thighs, spreading me wider. I'm soaked, and he knows it. His hungry eyes flick down, taking in every inch of me.

"Dave," I practically beg.

He positions himself at my entrance, the thick head of his cock teasing me for what's to come. I arch my back, pressing my hips up to meet him, desperate for him to fill me. Without warning, he pushes completely in and stars explode behind my eyes.

"Fuck," he groans out. I can feel him shaking with restraint from holding back.

"I need you to move," I say, wrapping my legs around his waist, pulling him deeper, my nails digging into his shoulder. "You won't break me."

Dave's growl is low and guttural as he begins to move, his grip on my waist will definitely leave a mark. Each thrust sends a new wave of pleasure shooting through me, and fuck, I'm so close. I know he is too as his thrusts become more erratic.

"You are so goddamn tight, baby." He grits out between each thrust.

"I'm close," I moan under his touch.

"I want you to come with me." He reaches between us, putting just enough pressure on my clit, causing me to thrash beneath his weight.

"Now," he groans, and I fall completely over the edge. My vision goes white as the most powerful orgasm I've ever had racks my body.

14
DAVE

I wake up to complete darkness. For a second, I think I'm in a coffin, but then my eyes adjust, and I take in my surroundings.

The room exudes a cozy warmth, far surpassing the comfort of my own. A green chair is positioned in the corner, accompanied by a lamp behind it. Next to the chair, there's a table cluttered with books. On the opposite side, there's a tall armoire with photos lining its top.

Movement draws my gaze downward, admiring the woman lying next to me. Sara has an arm and a leg draped over me, pinning me in place. Not that I mind; if I could wake up like this every day, I would be a happy man.

She shifts in her sleep, and her breast brushes my arm, sending a wave of awareness straight to my cock.

"Good morning, baby," I whisper into her ear.

"Good morning." A lazy smile spreads across her face. "What time is it?"

My gaze drifts to the clock on her nightstand. "It's seven."

"In the morning?" she yelps before burrowing her head into my chest.

A low chuckle escapes me. "Yes, in the morning."

"It should not be legal to wake up before noon." Her voice is indignant.

"Is that so?" I say as I roll her onto her back, my knees bracketing her hips, and let a little of my weight settle onto her, pinning her in place. I'm rewarded with a wide grin.

"Yes, especially on the weekend."

I smile, a wicked grin spreading across my face. "I bet I can make waking up fun for you."

"Oh, really, what do you have in mind?" she asks, her voice sultry.

"Well, I was thinking—breakfast in bed," I say, leaning down to kiss her neck.

She perks up. "Oh, I love that idea."

"I thought you might. Now I'm going to enjoy my meal, and then I'll make you yours."

———

I'm cooking a simple breakfast: waffles, eggs, and bacon, when Sara saunters into the kitchen, clutching the sloth I bought her to her chest. The sight of her makes me feel at ease and relaxed, but the guilt of not telling her the whole truth bubbles up again, but I shove it down, focusing on the moment instead.

"Wow," she says through a yawn, her voice still sleepy as she wraps her arms around my waist. "It smells amazing."

I turn, pulling her into a proper hug, holding her close. I breathe in her sweet and intoxicating scent. "Thanks," I murmur into her hair. "I learned from my Bubbe."

She scrunches her eyebrows together in confusion. It's so adorable.

"That's what I called my grandmother."

"Oh," she says with a soft smile, "you said 'called'..."

"Yeah," I take a sip of my coffee, averting my gaze. It never gets easier no matter how many times I've said it outloud. "She passed away a few years ago."

Her body stills for half a second before she tightens her hold on me. "Oh. I'm so sorry."

I close my eyes as she hugs me tighter, the comfort of her arms settling around me, and for a brief moment, the guilt eases—replaced by the ache of knowing how much this woman already means to me. It would be the perfect time to tell her everything. "Hey—" I try to start the conversation when she interrupts me.

"Would you like a cup of tea?" She slides out of my arms.

"I'll take some chamomile."

Sara freezes midway to the cabinet, "I didn't say I had chamomile." She looks at me suspiciously.

"Oh—I mean, I'd love some if you had it. It's my favorite type of tea." I say, quickly trying to recover from my slip-up.

"Oh, really? It's mine too," she replies excitedly. "I just got this new brand the other day. It's been one of my favorites."

"Hmm." I turn my focus to the stove so I don't accidentally let it slip that I was the one who picked up her new favorite tea.

Sara grabs a kettle from the cabinet, fills it with water, and places it on the burner next to the eggs. She hands me two plates from the cabinet, and I start plating our breakfast. Being here with her feels almost domestic, and I find that I am enjoying this feeling. I wish this was us every day.

"So, what do you have planned today?" she asks in between bites.

"I don't have anything planned." I smile at her, enjoying the food. It warms me to know she's eating more than cereal and canned tuna. "What did you have in mind?"

"Well, we could have a lazy day in, binge-watch some shows, and then maybe you could hang out and watch me stream tonight?" Her voice trails off at the end, like she's nervous.

"That sounds great to me." I brush a piece of hair behind her ear. "Don't be nervous, I'm excited to watch you in action."

"Thanks." She smiles softly. "Let me grab snacks and Sir Sloths-A-Lot, and we'll get started."

"Oh, is that his name?" I gesture to the sloth sitting beside her on the counter.

"Yup, he's my emotional support buddy."

I chuckle. "I knew you'd like him when I saw him." The moment the words were out of my mouth, my eyes instantly snap to hers.

Her eyes widen. "What do you mean when 'you saw him'?"

"I—" I start, but I'm at a loss for words.

She looks at me expectantly, her expression calm, her eyes giving nothing away.

I put my fork down, turning fully to her, and take a deep breath. *Just do it, rip it off like a band-aid.*

"I'm your DoorDash shopper," I confess, immediately cringing at the words.

"I'm sorry—what?" Her voice jumps an octave.

Clearing my throat, I stuff my hands into my pockets. "I'm the one who's been delivering to you these past few weeks."

Realization flashes across her face. "The soup?"

"I made it," I admit quietly. "I didn't think you should be eating canned soup while you were sick. I should've told you sooner—I know that—but—" I trail off when I really see her expression. The warmth drains from her eyes, replaced by anger.

"Get. Out."

"Sara, please." I take a step towards her, but she retreats.

"No." Her voice is steady, unyielding. "I want you out. Now."

Defeated, I gather my things and head towards the door, preparing for my walk of shame home. Before leaving, I turn back toward the kitchen, taking one last look at her. The pain in her eyes broke my heart.

I did that.

The feeling lingers with me all the way home.

15
SARA

The incessant knock on my door startles me awake. I blink the sleep from my eyes, my head feeling like it's about to explode. I eye the empty bottle of wine on my coffee table; that explains why my head feels like it's a ten-pound bowling ball.

Sydney's voice comes through the door. "Sara Mei Lin, you open this door right now, or I'm kicking it down." It's way too early for this. I glance at my phone—two-thirty in the afternoon—okay so *late* according to the societal norm.

Dragging my lifeless body to the door, I pull it open and squint up at Sydney. She's standing there like she's ready for a night on the town: black leather leggings, an oversized cropped sweater slipping off one shoulder, chunky gold hoops catching the light. Her long braids cascading down her back. She looks effortlessly put together in the way that makes me wish I were her right now.

"Girl," she says, pushing past me without waiting for an invitation. "I've been calling you *forever*. I thought you died."

"You're being dramatic," I mutter, shuffling toward the couch. "This is my normal wake-up time."

She snorts, toeing off her boots. "It's two-thirty. And I haven't heard from you in two days." Her eyes narrow when they land on the empty wine bottle on my coffee table. "Soooo, what happened with Dave?" She starts cautiously.

I hesitate, then sigh. "He's not who he seems to be."

Her entire body stills. "Okay..." She turns to face me fully. "What do you mean by *that*?"

"You remember the DoorDash delivery guy?"

Sydney's eyes light up. "Your oat milk savior?"

"Yes," I reply flatly. "Him. And Dave. Same person. Dave *is* him. Or he's also Dave. Two peas in a pod—or, in this case, one pea."

She blinks once. Then twice. "You're not making any sense, honey." She crosses her arms over her chest.

I tuck my legs under me, releasing an exaggerated sigh, and I start from the beginning. I tell her the fully detailed version, not just the bits and pieces I've been highlighting. I start with the oat milk, Sir Sloths-A-Lot, the homemade soup, and the morning after our night together. By the time I finish recapping the whole thing, Sydney is staring at me, dumbfounded.

"Wow. So that was a lot, I understand the wine now." She gestures dramatically to the bottle.

"You didn't recognize his picture on the app?" she tone dripping with skepticism.

"The guy on the app has a beard." I say, pulling out my phone to show her. It's not the first time I've tried zooming in on the tiny picture on DoorDash to justify my naivety. "I guess he's one of those guys where a beard drastically changes his face."

"Have you talked to him since? Get his side of the story?"

"No, I don't want to talk to him. There's nothing he can say that makes this okay." I know I sound irrational but he broke my trust. "I don't know if I can trust him," I admit softly. "He lied about who he was. And if he lied about that, what else could he lie about?" My chest tightens. "What if we get serious and he does it again?"

"Honey." Sydney sits beside me. "You can't let the fear of being hurt again make you shut the door on love."

"I'm not closed off," I say defensively.

She gives me a look. "It's been four years. And this is the first man I've seen you genuinely excited about. The first one who made you smile like that again."

I swallow. "I know. I think I'm just... scared."

She scoffs. "Of course you are. We all are." Then her face hardens. "But don't let—"

"Fuck Donald," I blurt. But my mind betrays me, dragging up memories I've worked hard to bury—*I'm working late. She's just a friend. You're being paranoid.* Months of white lies before I caught my ex with his coworker.

"Yes," she agrees immediately. "Fuck Donald. Don't let him ruin your faith in love."

She takes my hands. "When you find a connection like that, it's not you versus the guy. It's you versus your fear. And today could be the perfect day to resolve your fear."

I frown at her. "Today?"

"Sara," she huffs, like she's explaining something to a child, "it's Valentine's Day."

The words land with a dull thud. I blink, realization washing over me. I haven't celebrated Valentine's Day since the incident.

I sniff. "I don't even know where to start."

"Well," Sydney takes a breath, then stands and wrinkles her nose dramatically, "the *first* thing you need to do is take a shower."

"Hey!"

"Trust me," she says matter-of-factly. "Take a long shower. Maybe a bubble bath. Pamper yourself. Then we'll decide the next step."

I manage a small smile. "Bossy."

"You love it." She gives me a tight squeeze, and I can't help but lean into her comfort.

"Thanks, Syd." I sniff, wiping the tears that escape down my cheeks.

"Always."

Thirty minutes later, I emerge from my room like a new woman. My hair is washed and dried, my skin feels baby soft, and I'm starting to think Sydney *does* know what she's talking about.

"Okay," I say plopping down next to her on the couch. "What's next?"

"Well, now we realign your crystals."

"I don't have any crystals," I deadpan.

"Wrong." She pulls a purple velvet sachet from her bag. "You have crystals." She hands me the bag, looking at me like I should know what to do with it. "Now you need to imbue it with your energy. Take them out, and just hold on to them for a few minutes."

I follow her instructions and hold the crystals to my chest, squeezing them a bit harder than necessary. I channel all my positive energy into the vibrant rocks and silently pray that, by some miracle, they will transform my love life.

16

DAVE

I stare at the red heart circled on my rotation schedule on the fridge.

Saturday, February Fourteenth.

Valentine's Day.

Two days since I left her house in shame.

I'm surprised Sue hasn't called the neighborhood watch on me for the number of times I've walked back and forth in front of Sara's house.

I messed everything up. If only I had told her the first time I delivered... but then, would she have talked to me like she had been, or would she have put me in the neighbor box, and we never would have connected the same way? *At least, that's what I'm telling myself to ease the guilt.*

The vibration of my phone on the kitchen counter snaps me out of my self-pity fest. It's a DoorDash order request... from Sara. I rub my eyes, trying to convince myself that it's not playing tricks on me.

At first, I focus on the order request: flowers, chocolate, and one of those ridiculously huge stuffed animals you win at the state fair. My stomach twists. She's buying herself flowers? And chocolate? On Valentine's Day?

No. Absolutely not. And then I spot the note: "This is Sydney, fix it!"

Without a second thought, I accept the order. Sydney is throwing me a lifeline, and I intend to take it.

I head to the local florist first, grabbing a small vase of fresh peonies, carefully choosing the brightest reds and pinks I can find. Then I stop by the chocolate shop and pick up the largest heart-shaped box I can carry without knocking someone over. The stuffed bear sitting in my passenger seat almost looks like a person.

The closer I get to her house, my nerves get the better of me, and instead of pulling up to her place, I park at my own house. I take a deep breath, trying to calm my nerves—what's the worst that can happen? She slams her door in my face and I make a second walk of shame back to my house. This time— with a giant stuffed bear. Definitely not embarrassing at all.

My phone buzzes in my jacket and I pull it out to see it's a FaceTime call from my sister. I click accept to find that instead of seeing my sister's face, I'm looking at what appears to be a cheek. I hope it's a face cheek and not an ass cheek. The phone shakes for a few seconds before the culprit's face comes into view.

"Uncle Da!" my nephew shrieks from the other end of the line.

"Hey, Bubba," I say, smiling despite myself. "Does your mom know you have her phone?"

"Cry?"

"What? No, Bubba. I'm not crying."

"Cry! Cry!" he yells, and I hear the thudding of tiny feet as he takes off running. I'm hoping—praying—he's heading straight for his mom. Luca is only two; his vocabulary is... limited.

"Luca, did you take my phone?" my sister's voice comes through the speaker, followed by a gentle scolding. "You know you're not supposed to take my phone." She pauses. "Wait—what do you have there?"

A second later, her face appears on the screen, squinting as she tries to get a better look at me.

"Oh hey, Dave," my sister greets me at the same time Luca yells, "Cry!"

Eliana sighs, brushing toddler hair out of her son's face. "Sorry about that. He just learned that when someone is sad, they cry. He hasn't quite figured out the difference yet. So if he thinks you're sad, he just says, 'cry.'"

She studies me again. "So... are you sad?"

I hesitate, then let out a heavy sigh as I push open my front door and collapse onto the couch.

"Yeah. I messed things up with a girl I was... kind of seeing."

Her expression softens immediately. "The neighbor? Sara?"

I nod. "Yeah. The cute one I told you about. We were talking a lot, and I didn't exactly tell her the whole truth." I scrub a hand over my face. "It kind of blew up in my face."

"Oof." She cringes slightly, but her face is lined with empathy. "I'm sorry, sweetheart. But—" she gives me *the look* "—you know better than to lie to a woman."

"I didn't think it was a lie," I mumble. "More like... an omission."

She arches a brow. "Men always think that."

"I apologized," I add quickly. "She didn't want to talk to me."

"When did you try?"

"The same day she kicked me out of her house."

My sister winces. "Okay, yeah. That was probably too soon."

"So I should just... leave it alone?" I ask, even though I hate the idea.

"No," she chides. "You should try again. You gave her space, but now it's time to be honest. *Fully* honest. And don't do it because you want forgiveness. Do it because she deserves the truth."

I exhale slowly. "I'm just scared of what she'll say."

She smiles, soft but firm. "Life's scary, little bro. But the best things usually are. If she still says no, at least you'll know you did the right thing."

Luca suddenly pops into view, pressing his face against the screen. "Uncle Da... no cry?"

I chuckle, the ache in my chest fading a bit. "Yeah, Bubba. Uncle Da's okay."

Luca grins widely at my sister, before toddling off again.

Eliana laughs. "See? Even a two-year-old knows—you'll be fine. You should come by tomorrow for dinner. It'll be good for you."

"Yeah, I will. Thanks for the pep talk, Lana." I give her a small smile.

"Anytime." She replies before hanging up.

I give myself one last moment before I open my door, grabbing everything I purchased, and force my feet across the street. My heart is pounding so hard it feels like it's trying to escape my chest. I'm sure Sue is watching from her window, wondering what the hell I'm doing, but I don't care. I don't know what Sara will say or do, but I have to try.

I ring the doorbell, hiding behind the bear like it might give me courage.

"Dave?" Sara's voice is soft, surprised.

I peek around the bear and meet her gaze—those dark eyes filled with confusion, warmth, and something that looks dangerously close to forgiveness.

"Happy Valentine's Day," I say sheepishly. "I don't know

if you have plans, or if you're still mad... but I didn't want you to have to buy your own Valentine's Day gift." I swallow. "And I meant what I said the other night. You should be worshiped."

She blinks at me, clearly stunned. "Sydney..." she mutters under her breath.

"Yeah," I admit with a nervous laugh. "She told me to fix it. So... here I am. Trying to fix it."

Her smile wavers, and I know it's now or never.

"I'm so sorry I lied to you," I blurt, finally finding the courage to meet her eyes fully. "I've had a crush on you since the day you moved in." I let out a quiet chuckle. "Maybe more than a crush. I was a coward—I didn't ask you out when I should have. You completely blew me away. And I convinced myself there was no way a woman like you would want a guy like me, so I chickened out. I've regretted it ever since."

I take a breath and keep going. "When I realized you were the one I was delivering to, I took the opportunity to talk to you." I shake my head at myself. "It's a pretty far-fetched story —using a delivery app as a dating app—but it gave me access to you when you were unguarded, and I took the chance. I'm sorry if that made you feel manipulated. I never wanted to hurt you."

"It's a weird *How I Met Your Father* story," she jokes, fidgeting with the sleeves of her sweater. Then she adds quickly, words tumbling out, "Not that I'm saying you're the future father of my children."

I don't say it out loud, *but I want to be.*

"I think... I understand why you did it," she continues, her voice barely above a whisper. "Truth is, I've been pretty reclusive since I found out my ex cheated on me and moved out. Opening myself up to someone again hasn't been easy." She looks up at me, hopeful but cautious. "But I'm hoping we could try?"

"I'd like that," I answer without a single second of hesitation. "More than anything."

Her smile brightens. "Me too."

"So," I start, nerves flaring again, "will you be my Valentine?"

"She would love to!" Sydney yells from the couch.

Sara laughs, shaking her head. "She's right. I would love to."

And just like that, for the first time in years, *I have a Valentine.*

EPILOGUE - SARA

The next time I move, I'm planning better—and making absolutely sure it's not during the hottest month of the year in Eagleton. The boob sweat is next-level aggressive today.

Thank God the move itself is short.

Dave and I decided to move in together after a few months of dating. I love my little cottage, but his place had history, memories, and—most importantly—love flowing from every corner.

He wanted the house to feel like my home, so he spent the last month turning one of the spare bedrooms into my gaming room and library, refusing to let me see it until today—move-in day.

"Are you ready?" he asks, leading me up the stairs.

"Yes." I give his hand a little squeeze.

"I hope you love it." He opens the door, stepping back so I can take in the space.

It's *beautiful*. One wall is lined with floating shelves already stocked with my books—romance novels, fantasy paperbacks, collector's editions I thought were still packed away. A plush reading chair sits in the corner beneath a floor lamp with soft, golden light. My desk faces the window, my full PC setup already assembled, LED lights tucked discreetly behind the monitor and shelves, glowing faintly. There's even a small couch along the opposite wall, layered with blankets, pillows, and of course, Sir Sloths-A-Lot is watching over his kingdom.

"I love it!" I say, throwing myself at him. He catches me with ease, kissing my temple before setting me back down.

"I'm glad. This is your home now too. I want you to have everything you need."

"As long as I have you, that's all I'll ever need." I smile at him.

A choking sound from the hallway makes us both look over.

"Oh, I'm sorry, there was so much love in the air I couldn't breathe," Sydney teases, arms crossed as she surveys the room.

"Maybe you should go back to the house if you can't breathe here. I heard the air is better across the street," I toss back at her. Sydney's moving into my place now that I no longer need it.

"Ha ha, very funny."

"I can't believe your landlord could just kick you out like that."

"I guess since I was renting month-to-month, he had the right not to renew," she replies with a shrug. "Would've been nice to get more notice, though."

"Well," I smirk, "lucky for you, your best friend in the whole wide world just happened to be vacating her place."

She smiles at me. "I know. Thank you again. I really appreciate it."

"Of course. You're basically my sister." I wrap her in a tight hug.

"Just promise me you won't barge in unannounced," Dave chimes in behind me.

"No promises," Sydney sing-songs.

"Okay, I'll leave you two to chat." Dave chuckles, placing a gentle kiss on my forehead. "I'm heading downstairs to meet Aiden so he can assist in moving some of the heavier items. He mentioned that he's bringing brownies from Charlie's bakery."

"Yummmm!" I'm drooling just thinking about those brownies. "Thanks, babe."

"Anything for you," he says, leaning in for a kiss before leaving.

"You two are disgustingly adorable," Sydney teases, plopping down onto the couch.

"I know." I smile. "Who would've thought you could get love—delivered with DoorDash?"

ACKNOWLEDGMENTS

Thank you so much for reading Love, Delivered! I still can't believe Dave and Sara are finally out in the world. I'm a sucker for a unique meet-cute, and this one was calling to me when my toddler woke me up one night. I couldn't stop thinking about this story.

Fast forward to late nights, lots of coffee, and writing in between naps, and this story was ready for its debut.

There were so many people who made this book possible, and I truly cannot thank you all enough for your support and love. *Love, Delivered* would not be here today without each and every one of you!

To Leigh - aka Master Leigh, this story exist because of you. If not for your endless encouragement, late night edits, countless voice notes, graphic designs, and so much more. You are forever stuck with me and I'm so thankful soup and Cindy brought us together.

To Cindy - Thank you for being the sounding board to all the random thoughts in my head during this writing journey.

To Elena - I couldn't have found a better editor to help encourage and be open to my crazy schedule. I promise, I won't spring a new book on you in a month's time span.

To Lauren, Evelyn, Brittany, Karen, Paige, Elle, and Adelle - Thanks for reading *Love, Delivered* and providing your honest feedbacks.

To Gabriela, Mel - For the beautiful character arts. You brought the characters to life, and it makes my heart so happy my readers can enjoy it as much as I do.

To my husband, Peyton - Thank you for continuing to push me towards my dreams, but always staying close by to catch me if I fall. Without you, I would never have the courage to explore my writing journey.

To my ARC team - Thank you for supporting this indie author journey. Your messages, posts, stories, reviews, and comments truly make my day and I am so thankful to have you in my corner.

Finally, thank YOU. I am honored you decided to read *Love, Delivered*. I hope you enjoyed Dave and Sara's love story!

ABOUT THE AUTHOR

Writing under a pen name, Nora Lane is a Vietnamese romance writer, a mom, a wife, a pharmacist, and a coffee addict. She lives in Oklahoma, with her husband and two boys, but wishes to one day be in a state that doesn't experience all four seasons in one day.

Living in her own grumpy x sunshine, friends-to-lovers, workplace romance happily-ever-after, she writes short, sweet, and fun stories for readers who need a quick escape.

instagram.com/noralanewrites

tiktok.com/noralanewrites

threads.com/noralanewrites

ALSO BY NORA LANE

Tied Up for Love

He's tasked to pull off a kidnapping.
Fate gives him the wrong twin.

The absolute last thing book-obsessed Charlotte Bennett expects while browsing the bookstore is to be kidnapped by grumpy ex-Marine, Aiden Carter—the man tasked to abduct her twin sister.

Charlotte is forced into his vehicle with bound hands and a sack over her head, her heart tripping with nerves—the good and bad kind—while a scowly broad-shouldered man drives her into a panic.

When an unexpected stop allows Charlotte to get to know the man responsible for her abduction, the chemistry in the air charges with tangible proof of a dark romance gone right.

Suddenly, she starts to wonder if the man who tied her up could also be the one to win over her heart.